For my sister,
Jessie

First U.S. edition 2002

Library of Congress Cataloging-in-Publication Data
Freeman, Tor.
Roar! / by Tor Freeman. —1st U.S. ed.
p.   cm.
Summary: As she spends the day with her mother, reading, playing, doing
chores, and eating, a young girl imagines that she is various animals.
ISBN 0-7636-1773-3
[1. Imagination—Fiction. 2. Animals—Fiction.
3. Mother and daughter—Fiction.] I. Title.
PZ7.F8778 Rah 2002
[E]—dc21   2001052493

10 9 8 7 6 5 4 3 2 1

Printed in China

This book was typeset in OPTI Typewriter Special.
The illustrations were done in acrylic, watercolor,
and colored pencil.

Candlewick Press
2067 Massachusetts Avenue
Cambridge, Massachusetts 02140

visit us at www.candlewick.com

CANDLEWICK PRESS
CAMBRIDGE, MASSACHUSETTS

ROAR!

Tor Freeman

Last night,
Mom read Lotte
a story about
animals from her
favorite book.

When Lotte woke
up this morning,
she was a lion.

Lotte went
downstairs
and Mom said,
"Good morning."

"Lions don't say good morning.
ROAR!" Lotte said.

Next, when Mom
was sewing,

Lotte
turned into
a monkey.

Mom said, "Be careful not to trip."
"Monkeys don't trip.
ROAR!" Lotte said.

Then Mom and
Lotte played
hide-and-seek.
Lotte was an
elephant.

"Here I come!"
called Mom.

She couldn't
find Lotte
anywhere.

Lotte jumped out.
"ROAR!" she said.

After lunch
Mom had some
work to do.
Lotte was
a bear.

The bear and Mom watered
the plants together.

The bear and
Mom built a
tower together.

Mom said,
"Not too high
or it'll fall."

ROAR!

"No it won't.
ROAR!"
Lotte said.

But it did.

By dinnertime Lotte was a crocodile.
"Eat your vegetables," said Mom.

"Crocodiles don't like vegetables.
ROAR!" Lotte shouted.

After supper,
Lotte was still
a crocodile.

"Bedtime, Lotte,"
Mom said.
"Shall I carry
you upstairs?"

"I'm not Lotte! I'm a
crocodile," Lotte said.
"And crocodiles don't
like being carried
upstairs. ROAR!"

"Oh," said Mom. "I'm not sure
   I like crocodiles."

The crocodile
sat alone at the
bottom of the stairs.

Mom came and sat beside her.
"Crocodiles don't like being
carried upstairs," Mom said.
"But I know someone who does.
Do you?"

     "I think I do,"
        said the crocodile ...

Mom hugged
Lotte and
carried her
upstairs.

Lotte put
her pajamas on
all by herself.

"I'm glad you're
Lotte again,"
Mom said.

Then she read Lotte a story about
a little penguin from her favorite book.
Mom kissed Lotte good night.
"Sweet dreams, Lotte," she said.

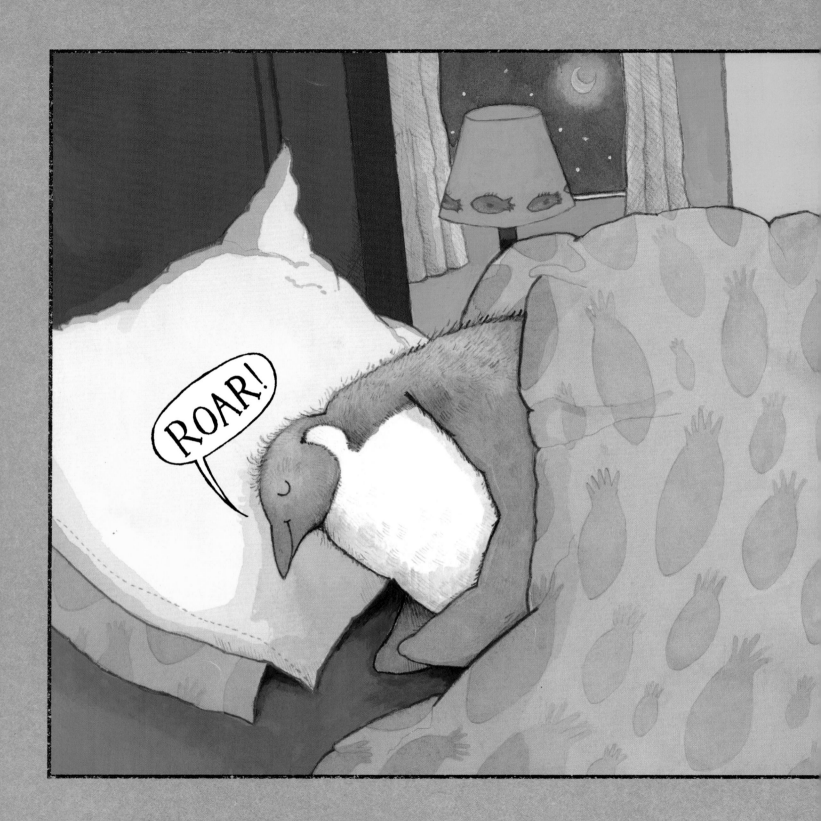

"ROAR!" Lotte said . . .

and she went to sleep.